W9-AJR-157

Copyright © 2006 by NordSüd Verlag, Gossau Zürich, Switzerland
English translation copyright © 2006 by North-South Books Inc., New York.

All rights reserved. No part of this book may be reproduced or utilized in any form
or by any means, electronic or mechanical, including photocopying, recording,
or any information storage and retrieval system, without permission
in writing from the publisher.

First published in the United States, Great Britain, Canada, Australia,
and New Zealand in 2006 by North-South Books Inc., an imprint
of NordSüd Verlag AG, Gossau Zürich, Switzerland.
Distributed in the United States by North-South Books Inc., New York.

Library of Congress Cataloging-in-Publication Data is available.
A CIP catalogue record for this book is available from The British Library.

ISBN-13: 978-0-7358-2084-5 / ISBN-10: 0-7358-2084-8 (trade edition)
10 9 8 7 6 5 4 3 2 1
ISBN-13: 978-0-7358-2085-2 / ISBN-10: 0-7358-2085-6 (library edition)
10 9 8 7 6 5 4 3 2 1

Printed in Belgium

MARCUS PFISTER

RAINBOW FISH
FINDS HIS WAY

TRANSLATED BY J. ALISON JAMES

NORTHSOUTH
BOOKS

NEW YORK / LONDON

Deep in the sea, a terrible storm was approaching.
Nearly all of Rainbow Fish's friends had taken shelter
in their protective cave. Only the little striped fish and
Rainbow Fish were still swimming about.

"Come on," the little striped fish said, "we have to go
back to the others. We're only safe from the storm if
we're in the cave!"

"You go on ahead," Rainbow Fish said. "I'm almost
finished collecting these wonderful blue pebbles. I'll be
right there."

"Hurry, please!" The striped fish didn't want to leave his friend. "It is far too dangerous out here in the open."

But Rainbow Fish was too busy to be afraid.

Just as he was gathering one last pebble, the storm hit. He tried to swim against the rushing water, but it was too strong. A whirling current of water tore through with such force that Rainbow Fish was whipped against a rock and suddenly everything went black. Then the current swept him away.

When he could finally see again, the storm was over.
Dazed, he looked around. The water was so cloudy that
he couldn't see the fins of any of his friends. As the
water cleared, he realized that it wasn't just the water—
he had no idea where he was.

Suddenly Rainbow Fish backed into something prickly.

"Ouch! Watch where you're swimming," grumbled
a voice.

Rainbow Fish looked to see who had spoken. It was a spiky puffer fish, hidden among some water cactus. "My, oh my, who have we here? I've never seen you in these parts before."

"That's because I've never been here before," Rainbow Fish said. And he told how the storm had dragged him away from his friends.

"Do you have any idea how I can find my way back?" Rainbow Fish asked. "My friends all have a glittering silver scale, like this one."

"A glitter school," said the puffer fish. "How unique. But no, I have no idea. Never seen a scale like that in my life. What if I take you to my friend the scallop. She gets around more than I do. Maybe she can help you."

The scallop listened calmly to the problem. She thought for a long time, cleared her throat, and finally said, "The only school of fish around here is a school of striped fish. But there's not a glittering scale among them."

"Striped fish?" Rainbow Fish perked up. "One of my friends is a striped fish!"

"Well then," said the scallop, "I'll take you to them."

"Excuse me for asking," said Rainbow Fish, "but how can you take me there? You don't have fins to swim with."

"Just you watch!" The scallop suppressed a smile.

Before Rainbow Fish knew what was happening, the scallop was on her way. She snapped the two sides of her shell together and shot through the water as fast as Rainbow Fish could follow.

"Here we are," the scallop said, sounding pleased with herself. Rainbow Fish looked around. They were in the middle of a strange undersea landscape. It reminded him of a limestone cave and made him a little nervous.

"Excuse me," he said to the scallop. "But where are all the striped fish?"

"Come on out, everybody," called the scallop. "He's harmless."

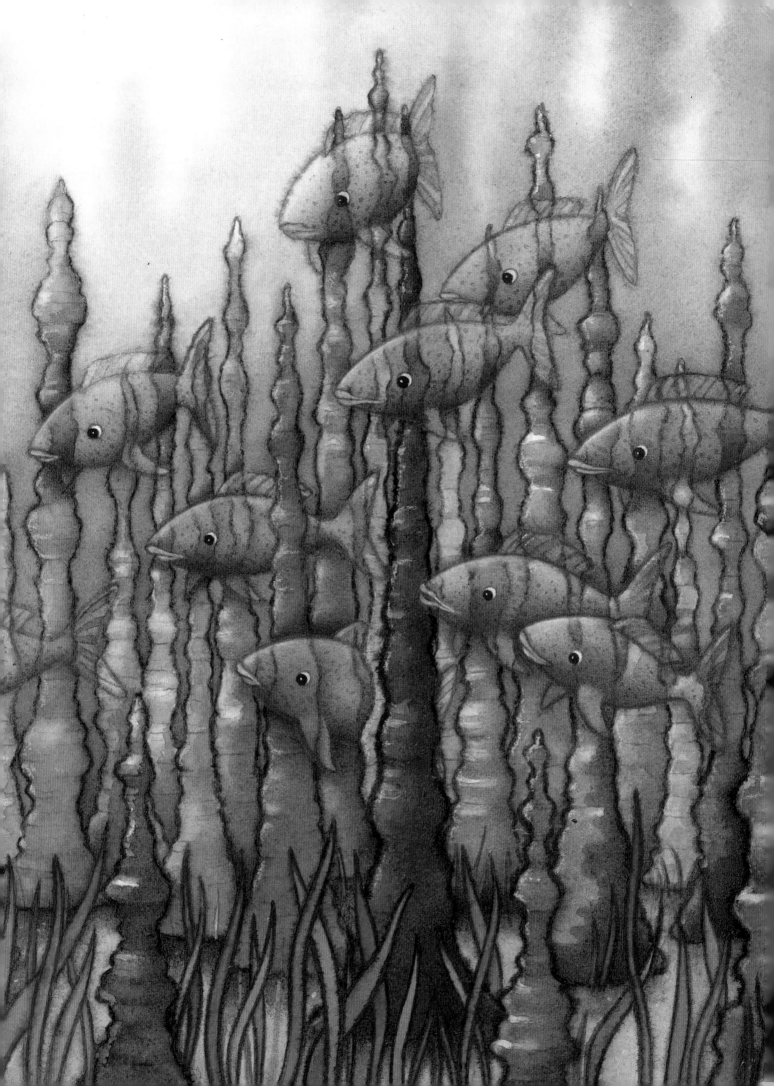

Timidly, the striped fish began to appear. They had hidden themselves well. Now Rainbow Fish could see more and more of them.

"But you're not green at all!" He looked at the fish with disappointment. "Now I'll never find my way home."

"Green?" asked a striped fish. "You mean green with gold stripes—like our cousins?"

"That's right," Rainbow Fish said, surprised.

"Well, we know where to find them. We'll take you right over to their school," said the fish.

From a distance, Rainbow Fish already recognized
the school of green-and-gold striped fish. They looked
exactly like his friend. The little striped fish had lived with
Rainbow Fish and his friends ever since he'd gotten
separated from his own school.

The green-striped fish were delighted when Rainbow
Fish told them that their long-lost brother was safe and
well. But when Rainbow Fish asked for help finding
his home, they had no idea at all where to direct him.

With a heavy heart, Rainbow Fish realized that he would have to search the ocean on his own until he found his friends.

He felt something poking him under his fin. What was that?

It was one of the blue pebbles that he had been gathering before the storm. "Here," said Rainbow Fish to the school, "you should have this to remember your brother. He and I were collecting these when I got caught in the storm." He gave the pebble to the fish.

One of the oldest striped fish came forward and looked closely at the stone. "I've seen this type of stone before," he said. "They're quite rare—they can only be found in one place. I've found such pebbles in the past. I know right where they are."

For a moment it was utterly still.

Then everyone began to swim around Rainbow Fish and bubble with excitement. They could help him after all!

Together they raced to the bed of blue pebbles where they saw Rainbow Fish's friends out searching for him. Of course the little striped fish was among them.

And so it happened that the two schools of fish were reunited with their long-lost friends at last. That night they all had a party to celebrate. They had so much fun that they would all remember it for years and years to come.

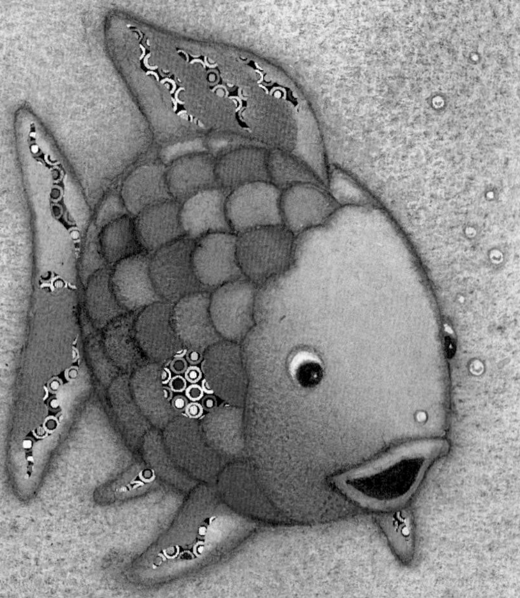